ATTILA, LOOLAGAX AND THE EAGLE

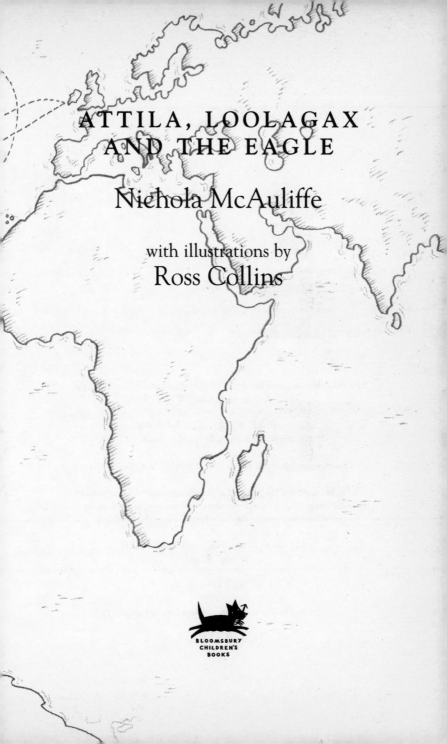

ATTILA, LOOLAGAX AND THE EAGLE

Nichola McAuliffe

with illustrations by
Ross Collins

BLOOMSBURY
CHILDREN'S
BOOKS

First published in Great Britain in 2003 by Bloomsbury Publishing Plc,
38 Soho Square, London, W1D 3HB

Text copyright © Nichola McAuliffe 2003
Illustrations copyright © Ross Collins 2003

A CIP record of this book is available from the
British Library

ISBN 0 7475 6499 X

Printed in Great Britain by Clays Ltd, St Ives plc

10 9 8 7 6 5 4 3 2 1

For Peter Dagleish Bond
a king among penguins

Preface

NOW some years ago the pigeon had a hole named after it; the Pigeon-hole. And Man decreed that all things must fit into a Pigeon-hole. This meant that Rules must be Obeyed, and each creature was given its own set of Rules. For instance, if you were a fish then you must have gills and live in water.

'But,' said the fish, 'some of us don't only live in water and can breathe air out of the sky.'

'Ah!' said Man, 'then you are a lung fish.'

There was no escape, even for Men themselves.

The Rules said, if you live in a house with two children and a wife, work in an insurance firm and drive an estate car, you cannot possibly be a ballet dancer. But inside you may be a ballet dancer even if you weigh fifteen stone and have a wooden leg.

That is the way Pigeon-holes work and everything is forced to fit into one. But this is the story of creatures who didn't fit and what happened to them.

By the way, all the pigeons I know think they should be called Man-holes and are thinking of Getting Up a Petition.

Chapter One

So, there was a penguin. An aquatic bird that doesn't fly in the air, the most beautiful creature on earth when flying beneath the seas, but possibly a trifle inelegant walking.

They live on the southern end of the world where ice floes bump into each other on their way to being glaciers. As little more than an egg, this particular penguin, called Attila, would sit on the ice watching very little happen. The Antarctic's that sort of place. Then one day in a howling gale, he pottered up to his mother. She was chatting to about five hundred other penguins about the quickness of fish and how things had changed since her day.

'Mum,' he said.

'Yes Attila?' she said, squinting at him through the wind and snow.

'Mum, am I a penguin?'

Hearing this, about two hundred and fifty of her friends fell silent and stared.

'Are you a penguin?' his mother repeated, stunned. 'Is the water wet? Of course you're a penguin!'

Attila could see she was embarrassed in front of the other penguins, but he persisted.

'I'm not an ostrich?'

'No dear, you're not an ostrich.'

'How about a parrot?'

'You're NOT a parrot.'

'Well, might I have just a touch of peacock?'

'Listen,' said his mother, gritting her beak, 'I'm a penguin, your father's a penguin, even Auntie

10

Ethel, odd though she may have been, was a penguin. So you're a penguin. Clear?'

'Thanks, Mum,' he said, and went to find his Father.

Father was basking in a passing blizzard.

'Hallo, Father,' the small penguin shouted.

'Speak up Attila, bit of a blizzard blowing up!' said Father, ruffling his feathers a bit.

His son took a deep breath.

'Father, am I a penguin?'

'Of course you are.'

He took another deep breath.

'Not an ostrich or a parrot or even half peacock?'

'Look here,' said his father, 'you come from a long unbroken line of pure penguins. I am Jeroboam Pen Guin, your grandfather was Nebuchadnezzar Pen Guin and your great grandfather was Methuselah Pen Guin. You were named after your mother's side of the family, Attila Genghis Pen Guin. All right? Your mother can trace her family back to the Ice Age. You are therefore, without doubt, a penguin.' He paused. 'Why do you ask?'

Attila hesitated, then said, 'Well, it's just that if

I'm a penguin why do I hate the snow, and most of all . . . why am I always SO COLD?'

The shock to his father was so great that he fell over and hit his head on a migrating narwhal, who apologised.

He flipped back out of the water, shaking with anger.

'You CANNOT be cold!' he shouted. 'You're making it up,' he raged. 'It's disgusting, unnatural. Cold? A child of mine, a . . . a . . .' he spluttered, unable to encompass the enormity of his son's apparent perversion.

'Do you realise the disgrace to the family if this gets out!?'

He stumped up and down awhile, then suddenly he stopped and turned on his terrified son. He leaned very close and whispered frantically, 'You haven't talked to anyone else about this, have you? Well? Well?'

His voice had risen from a horrified whisper to a bark.

'N . . . No . . . just Mother, but I didn't tell her I was . . .'

The small frightened penguin barely spoke the last word: cold.

'And you never will!' Father was triumphant. 'I never want to hear another word of this unnaturalness. Disgusting! Flying in the face of nature! Not another word, mind.'

So saying, he launched himself into a crashing wave and his son was left alone with his guilty secret.

Attila stood looking at all those happy, normal penguins warmly diving in and out of the icy water and he realised, with a great wash of sadness, that he was different, and it seemed to him that was a very, very bad thing to be indeed.

A tear rolled down his cheek and froze there. He waddled away across the unfriendly white landscape until, in the distance, the great penguin tribe, each individual indistinguishable from the next, appeared to be a vast moving black carpet.

He felt very small and very alone and his little pink feet were very, very cold. As he stood there not knowing what to do, but knowing that he had finally run away, a head appeared in a hole in the ice.

It was enormous, brown all over, and it had vast liquid eyes above a great bristling moustache, which completely covered its mouth. Either side of this magnificent growth, two tusks, yellow with age, curved down to a massive chest. The big, gentle eyes regarded him and seemed to fill with tears at the sight.

'Oh dear! Little chap,' the great creature rumbled. 'Poor little penguin. What is it? What's the matter?'

Attila had heard it said that a walrus could never bear to see another creature in distress, and this, his first meeting with one, seemed to prove it. For the mountain, now patting him kindly about the head with a great barnacled flipper, was indeed a walrus.

Scarred and ravaged by a hundred years in the terrible seas, the walrus's eyes were the kindest Attila had ever seen in his small life. The penguin took a hiccoughing breath, pretending not to cry. 'I'm . . . I'm . . .'

He stopped, then a little too loudly and a little too fast he said, 'I'm cold! I was always cold. I'm not being silly. I won't grow out of it. I was born like it and that's the way I am.' Then he added, rather unnecessarily, 'So there!'

After a pause the walrus said, 'Is that all?'

'Yes,' Attila whispered miserably.

'I see.'

The walrus rumbled to himself awhile and gazed across at the gossiping penguin tribe.

'Well, well little chap,' he said eventually, 'it's not a sin or a crime, you know. There are many, many creatures who hate the cold.'

Attila couldn't believe what he was hearing.

'Hate the cold?' he repeated stupidly.

'Yes indeed, there are places where the snow has never fallen and where it's so hot that only stones can live.'

This was too much for a small penguin. He sat down with a bump, pink feet flapping feebly.

After a moment, the walrus said, 'Why don't you join me and my lady cousin on a little trip to Warmer Wetters. Perhaps you'll find others like you. After all, you can't be the only Oddbod in the world.'

And so it was that Sir Effluent Scrummage, the Venerable Walrus, with his cousin the Garrulous Sea Cow, with a Kind Heart, a Wonderful Chuckle and an Important Nose, called Lady Honoria Wette Bannister, the sea cow that is, not the nose, showed a small and frightened penguin the world.

Chapter Two

THEY set off north through the freezing southern ocean to find the deepest sea on earth.

'Because,' said the sea cow, 'there we will find wise creatures who will tell us where to find a place for you to live, a place where you will be free to be cold or hot or nothing at all and no one will say you're wrong.'

Attila knew better than to argue, though inside he doubted it.

So on they swam, further and deeper, the walrus telling tales of sea battles a hundred years before when he had seen men fall into the sea with no hope of salvation, and how they quietly died and the walruses mourned them as brothers.

The sea cow hummed a little tune to herself, her great nose wobbling with vibrato and her tiny little soprano voice rippling the water around her.

On and on they swam. The water was deeper, darker, colder than Attila had ever seen. It was so still it seemed to rest on their heads, pressing them to the black banked bottom.

After more hours than there are in several days, Sir Effluent said, 'Humph!'

And because it was so dark, Attila could not see why.

Then Lady Honoria said, 'Ooomph!'

Then Attila said, 'Oops!'

And there they sat on the floor of one of the deepest seas on earth. They sat for the longest moment in the thick darkness, then a voice said:

'Well, I'll be a pickled herring! Over Wetters!'

Which is a slightly rude name for Shallow Sea Swimmers, a bit like calling a policeman Mr Plod.

But neither the name nor the darkness disturbed Sir Effluent's exquisite manners. He offered his enormous flipper in the direction of the voice, saying, 'How do you do. Scrummage and party. We come seeking The Crustacean.'

The flipper hovered, ignored. But slowly light, glimmering tiny light, began to grow.

All around them, as far as the eye could see, was a carpet of tiny shrimps, each one fanning the water with a fringe of well-shaped legs and each one lighting up a tiny space with its own phosphorescence.

As they watched, more and more shrimps came out of the sand and the light grew and spread like warmth. The leading shrimp, more a petite prawn really, smiled and waved several legs.

'We are the Army of Illumination,' he said proudly. 'Like it?'

Lady Honoria sighed with delight, blowing away several hundred of the tiny living lights.

'Oh, I'm terribly sorry!' she said, attempting to

field a few with a flipper. 'I've never seen anything so beautiful. Quite magnificent.'

The leading shrimp, whose name was Ossian, simpered modestly.

'Oh, it's nothing,' he murmured, gesturing the party forward over the blanket of lights.

They swam to a cave of purple crystal which glimmered and glowed by the light of the army. The cave was not very deep, narrow at the entrance, widening out and then narrowing again at the back where a huge smooth black stone called an onyx made a throne for the largest and undoubtedly oldest lobster in the world.

His shell was sapphire blue and scarred with deep lines from fishermen's attempts to capture him. He rose and spoke in an old, old voice, heavy with memories of France.

'I am Herbert Langoustine. Centuries ago I escaped from the cages and the nets of men and here I have my kingdom where all creatures of the sea can claim sanctuary from persecution. How can I help you?'

Sir Effluent explained the problem over seaweed

and coral milk. The visitors were only sorry they hadn't arrived earlier as it is a wonder to see coral being milked.

Hours went by while the lobster pondered in silence.

The tiny shrimps fell asleep and their lights went out one by one. Suddenly the lobster clicked his ancient claws and out of the floor, or so it seemed, glided the biggest, ugliest fish the three had ever seen.

It was grey and lumpy, with burning red eyes and what looked like a droopy green lamp-post sticking out of the middle of its knobbly flat head. At the end of this strange growth was a brilliant bulb, about two hundred and forty watts, the walrus thought, which lit up the cave brightly. Indeed it shone so brightly that it woke the shrimps who all looked guilty and pretended they'd been awake all along.

The Ugly Fish positioned himself by the lobster, who adjusted the lamp and put on his reading glasses.

'Don't be deceived by appearances Attila,

Fumidor is not as fearsome as he looks. Are you?' said Herbert Langoustine.

The Ugly Fish blushed quite red under his lamp and stammered in a very pleasing tenor, 'I d-d-do do hope not. I think ind-d-deed. I'm not a b-bad looking chap, for a lamp fish.'

'Oh, by any standards!' cooed Lady Honoria, fluttering several of her chins.

The Ugly Fish, overcome by this feminine appreciation, nearly blinded everyone with the brightness of his lamp.

At this moment Herbert Langoustine's secretary arrived with papers, pens, reference books and bits of half-eaten seaweed held in several of his arms.

He was an octopus and obviously a very nervous one as he kept dropping things and talking to himself in a remarkably strong Spanish accent.

Herbert Langoustine then dictated a letter, which the octopus wrote in triplicate, all at the same time. Octopuses being a trifle deaf, it was a rather lengthy process, until Sir Effluent handed him a conch shell down which Herbert

Langoustine yelled and things speeded up considerably. The letter said:

> From Herbert Langoustine to the Great Iguana of the Galapagos Islands, greetings. The bearer of this letter is a penguin named Attila Genghis Pen Guin, rejected by his society and family. In the name of the unloved, help him and shelter him. May the salt be in your skin for ever. Your brother in need.

The letter was sealed with a melted pearl provided by a bashful oyster who giggled a lot.

Then Herbert Langoustine turned to Attila and said,

'Little penguin, my kingdom is not what you want, with its cold and darkness. You must find your way to the Galapagos Islands off the west coast of South America, near   land of Ecuador. There you will find a w;   warm hearts. It is the place fc   different. Now go on the New Ti on your side. It is a long and dangerous journey.'

They prepared to leave and Lady Honoria made a date to meet Fumidor on the continental shelf. He was so overcome with joy that his lamp exploded and he swam into a wall. The octopus waved a selection of arms, dropped all his papers and swirled off in a cloud of ink. Herbert Langoustine smiled his wise old smile. Sir Effluent, leading the way, carefully handed the letter to Attila and off they went.

The seas grew lighter and warmer, fish in brilliant coloured shoals swam by, chatting and laughing.

A shark expressed an interest in Attila until Sir Effluent threatened to convert him into a pair of high-heeled boots with matching handbag. The shark paled slightly and ate a passing eel, which gave him indigestion and made him grumpy for several days.

Then the storm hit.

It started with a wind which pulled the surface of the sea into great towers and angry craters. The dived, dived down below the waves, but a great whirlwind screamed by and took a great slice of sea, the bit in which they swam, lifted it a hundred feet into the air, threw it round and round, then spat it out in all directions.

As Attila flew through the terrible air he saw a rock exposed by the churning waters and knew he was going to hit it.

And he did.

Chapter Three

M ANY days later the penguin awoke looking up into a grey sky which was raining on him. Everything, even his feathers, hurt. There was no walrus and no sea cow. Then a voice said, 'Crumbs, mate, I thought you was a goner. Fancy a pilchard?'

Painfully, Attila turned his head and saw a seagull sitting on the quiet water nearby.

One eye was closed. His beak had chunks

missing from it and he had only one leg. His name, he said, was Basher from Bangor.

'I work the ferries see? Swansea to Cork and back, know what I mean? Wales, Ireland, Wales, leeks and potatoes, man, leeks and potatoes, see my meaning?'

'Where am I?' gasped Attila, not without a struggle as his tongue seemed welded to the roof of his beak.

'Just off the west coast of Ireland, see? Lovely spot. Bit wet mind, but we don't mind that, do we?' The seagull laughed and overbalanced so that only his one leg and tail showed. He came up chewing a bit of inner tube. 'Come on, man, let's get you off that rock.'

They paddled quite slowly for a while and fetched up on a long flat spit of sand. The sea was calm and it was raining. 'Soft day, mate, soft day. Dim problem. No problem,' Basher kept saying.

Chapter Four

AT the top of the sand dunes sat a small castle from which, though they did not know it, they were being watched.

'Is that a penguin?' said the man in the castle.

He was not tall or short and was a little podgy around the middle. His shirt, which was blue, was rumpled and his trousers hung from his stomach in a rather bored way. But his face was interesting. Under dark glossy hair his face was quite long but disguised by a neat beard and moustache just around his mouth and chin. He smiled a lot but because his teeth were bad he did not open his lips much. Above all this were eyes you could hardly see, the lids being like slits in pastry, but if you looked closely they glittered as if made of slivers of black glass. His name, which was to become only too well known to Attila, was Mochin, the 'ch' pronounced like the 'ch' in 'loch'. Mochin Accord.

He put his arm around the shoulders of his companion and said, 'Yes it is. It is!'

Then turning from the window, Mochin Accord said quietly and reasonably, 'Now, Percy, I'd like you to get me that penguin.' Mochin never raised his voice and was never unreasonable. He went on: 'I don't mind how you get it but I want it in my menagerie, behind bars, caged up for the world to stare at! Caged so the world will pay me for the pleasure I bring them. What do you think?'

Percy, still under the weight of Mochin Accord's arm, pulled himself up to his full height and tried to look evil, which is very difficult when you're only five feet two inches tall and built like a Christmas pudding. This then was Percy Demosthenes Pond, and he was chief catcher to Mochin Accord: Millionaire Collector and Killer of Animals.

Chapter Five

MEANWHILE, the seagull left to go about his business. He had flown about for some time searching for Sir Effluent and Lady Honoria but had found nothing so large or so amiable as those two.

Having thanked the seagull and said goodbye, Attila plodded up the road from the beach towards some hedges. As he neared them he heard sounds of distress. Close to the hedges was a sign which read: ANIMALS FOR SALE. FEW LEFT.

Rusty cars lined the pathway and men in check suits led sad goats to different trailers even though the goats were saying quite plainly that they didn't want to be separated. They cried as they were forced up ramps into filthy trailers.

A dirty little boy had a box of rabbits which he opened. The rabbits ran away and he shot them with an airgun. The rabbits asked him not to.

Attila was so frightened that he waited until it was all quiet and the people had gone before he moved. The last man to leave took away a parakeet with a cough which tried to sing 'Home Sweet Home' and appear cheerful.

The penguin crept forward and looked closely at the cages. All were rusty, smelly and dirty, and were now empty but for two donkeys who said they were being sent to be made into cat food the next day. Next to them, in the dirtiest cage of all, sat a huge, dusty pile of black feathers.

The creature was very thin, and every time it moved a feather fell off. It didn't speak and Attila didn't dare break the silence because he was pretty sure that this was a vulture and he had heard that vultures would eat anything just so long as it was dead or nearly so. Desperate to prove that he was neither, the penguin panicked and said, 'Good evening' in what he hoped was a lively tone.

At that moment a little girl come up. A little smiling brown girl with cuts on her knees and huge sticky-out ears. Attila saw her too late to run away. Petrified, he stood while she walked right round him.

'Hallo,' she said eventually. 'Would you be one of them penguins?'

Attila stared back dumbly, then nodded. The little girl said no more but went over to the donkeys and scratched their noses lovingly. Attila thought that was a friendly thing to do and relaxed a bit. She said to the donkeys:

'You know fellas, that Mochin Accord is a terrible wicked man, treating yous like this, after all the good service you've done. Ach, he's more bends than a corkscrew, so he has.'

So saying, she undid the cage and let the donkeys out. 'I'm taking you to me Grandma, she won't let that Mochin Accord turn you into cat food. She's a magical woman and won't she know what's to be done with you?'

The donkeys stood patiently by while the girl went to the vulture's tiny cage. She had just undone it when Percy D. Pond burst through the bushes brandishing a stick and net.

'What do you think you're doing?' he shouted, beating the girl with the stick. 'These animals are private property! That'll teach you to steal!'

With each word he flailed the stick at the girl but she was too quick and with tiny but expert movements she avoided each blow. Just as Percy was about to give up, one swipe with his stick caught the girl and sent her flying into a prickly gorse bush, making her cry out with surprise and pain.

At that, as if coming back to life, the vulture burst from his cage, unfurled his enormous black wings and, eyes flashing with fury, flew at the horrified Percy D. Pond.

For a moment Percy D. Pond stood, stick raised, bowler hat firmly planted on his round bald head, then he disappeared beneath a cloud of angry black feathers. As he fell he struck his head and lay unconscious under the furious talons of the vulture.

Attila and the girl thought that would be the end of Mr Pond, but no, the vulture simply hunched himself up on a nearby hummock and stretched out his long putty-coloured neck as if not knowing what to do next. The girl took over.

'Well aren't you the little smilin' fella?' she said to the vulture. 'I'm grateful to you. Now then, you'd best be going and so had we, before this terrible man wakes up and does more bad stuff.'

So saying, she and the donkeys disappeared into the drizzle.

In the mud, Percy D. Pond's wallet had spilled open, showing cards with his name and a picture of a Chinstrap Penguin with instructions on how to catch it, complete with diagrams, and how to keep it in captivity.

Attila realised that the man was going to want to put him in one of those cages when he awoke.

The vulture and the penguin were now very much in the same predicament. Shyly the little bird looked at the big one. To Attila's astonishment, the vulture was crying. Huge tears rolled down his curved beak and dripped on to the ruff at the bottom of his neck.

'I can't stand violence,' he said by way of explanation.

Attila offered him a pilchard to cheer him up.

'No thank you,' he said. 'I'm a vegetarian.'

Before Attila could think of anything to say, the vulture went on, 'I know! I know! It's not natural. You don't have to tell me. Goodness knows I've tried to eat meat. But there it is. My family threw me out because I was a disgrace to them and I ended up here. So . . . there it is.'

Carefully, still respectfully aware of the size of the vulture's beak, the penguin told him his story. The vulture listened in silence, then said, 'I'm not the only one then. Oooh, that is nice to know. Sorry, how do you do? Zophyloty Loolagax.'

Loolagax held out his wing. The penguin responded with his flipper.

'Attila Pen Guin, how do you do? I'm sorry about your friends.'

'Perhaps,' the vulture suggested shyly, 'we should team up. That is, if you don't mind,' he added hastily. 'We could perhaps try to get to the Galapagos Islands together. You could explain about Sir Effluent and Lady Honoria and the letter and . . . and well . . . the . . . er . . . Great Iguana might help us both.'

He ended even more shyly. Attila was so thrilled not to be alone any more that he almost hugged Loolagax but thought maybe that wasn't the way a Bird of the World should behave.

After a moment the vulture said carefully, 'Pardon me for saying this, but you can't fly, can you?'

'And you can't swim,' Attila replied a trifle defensively.

'Perhaps,' said Loolagax quickly, 'you could help me, maybe give me a tow now and then in the water, and I'll do the same for you in the air.'

And so the great friendship began. They made some hasty trial flights with Attila on the back of the vulture but he just slid off. Time was getting on and they were becoming frightened as Pond would be awake again soon.

In a moment of inspiration, one of them, neither of them could ever be sure who, decided to try to use Pond's braces.

It was difficult getting Pond out of them but they managed it and Loolagax put the back ends which are quite close together in his beak and Attila put the button holes on the other, far apart ends, on the tips of his flippers. Attila then stood behind Loolagax, flippers outstretched in a sort of flying position. But when the elastic was pulled tight Loolagax couldn't keep hold of his end and the braces snapped back, hitting the penguin on the beak.

They needed something like the bit on a horse's bridle to keep the braces in the vulture's mouth and soon found an old-fashioned key sticking out of the lock of one of the cages.

They put the round end through one button hole on the tip of the braces and the knobbly end through the other, then the vulture took the key in his mouth with the braces going back like reins to Attila's outstretched flippers, and, comfortable in his new harness, slowly moved off.

The braces became taut, the elastic pulled tight and the penguin began to run along as fast as his little pink legs would go. After a longish sprint by penguin standards, the vulture was flying along about two feet off the ground and Attila, flippers locked flat, levelled out his body and rose off the ground. The first Penguin Glider was launched.

Attila's tummy bumped along the ground a bit at first, but they flew quite steadily for about a mile before they decided to try a landing, at which point they crashed into the side of a large hump sticking out of an otherwise flat landscape.

The hill was undamaged, and as they nursed their bruises the two friends congratulated themselves on the success of their maiden flight. Nothing could stop them now.

Far enough from immediate danger and completely exhausted, they slept dreaming hopeful dreams.

Chapter Six

LIFTING himself from the mud, Percy D. Pond picked up his bowler hat, checked that his half-moon glasses were undamaged and limped back to the castle.

'Beaten up?' Mochin Accord's voice was quiet but deadly. 'You were beaten up?'

He looked at Pond, who was dripping mud on to his priceless carpet, with contempt.

'You were beaten up by a vulture?'

His voice was so quiet, so reasonable. Pond looked down at the pool in which he stood in shame.

'Yes, sir,' he whispered.

'Well?' inquired Accord with menacing friendliness. 'What now?'

'Sir, I think, before I passed out altogether, that I heard them say they were heading for the Galapagos Islands,' said Pond.

There was a cold heavy silence, like yesterday's custard.

'Well, off you go then,' said Mochin Accord reasonably. 'Get after them.'

'Yes, sir,' said Pond, executing a smart about turn and falling flat on the carpet with his trousers round his ankles.

'Um . . . no braces,' he mumbled, trying desperately not to be there.

'Get out,' said Mochin pleasantly.

In the morning the sun came up making the two birds feel warm and happy.

Loolagax stretched his long featherless neck and in doing so spotted something above them on a rocky ledge. Curious to meet anyone who could guide them to the Galapagos they climbed up and saw that it was an eagle's nest. Cautiously, Attila and the vulture approached it. Both of them knew that eagles can be quite touchy, and if they get upset they usually eat you.

They peered over the edge of the eyrie, and there in the bottom was a small, four-legged creature with a pointy nose, bright button eyes and lots of sharp spines.

'Good morning,' it said in a dignified way. 'Who are you?'

They told him and politely asked who he was.

'Me? I am the Eagle.'

Neither Attila nor Loolagax liked to say anything, but both of them had their doubts.

'You don't believe me, do you?' The creature's voice rose to an outraged squeal. 'Well, I'll show you!'

With that he assumed a flying position and launched himself at a flock of sheep grazing some distance below, intending to grab one by the neck and lift it back to the nest for breakfast.

The sheep took it very well. They were used to

being attacked in this way and, having stepped out of the way, very kindly picked the little creature out of the crater he had made in their pasture and asked if he was all right.

'All right? Of course I'm all right, you stupid sheep. I was just testing. But next time . . . watch out!'

The sheep ignored this rudeness and offered him some grass. Turning his back on them he stamped back up the mountain towards the others. When he finally puffed up to them he said, 'I don't fly up. I need the exercise.'

This stopped Attila and Loolagax asking any further questions.

Over a few berries and some sheep milk, which his downstairs neighbours had given him to stop him starving, the Eagle told his visitors about himself.

He had been born in Bavaria, near Munich, which is a town in Germany. Shortly after his birth his mother and father were run over by a car and he was bundled into a box and sent away to be sold in a pet shop.

The people who bought him wanted him sent to England to be a pet for their twins who were at school there, but England had very strict laws keeping animals out because of a disease called rabies so, instead of putting him in quarantine for six months, which is what the English law required, they tried to smuggle him in, on a ship bound for Liverpool.

Just outside the port, the customs men came aboard. They're like policemen, only more strict.

The people smuggling the Eagle panicked and threw him overboard, box and all.

He bobbed about for days until the box was broken when the sea washed it on to the rocks of the Irish coast.

The creature staggered ashore and was rescued by an old, blind sheepdog, named Seamus.

Seamus was a grand dog, a champion in his time and even though almost too old to walk, stone blind and not a little deaf, he resolved to take care of the foundling as best he could.

First he tried to find out what it was that had been washed up on the rocks. All the creature would say was, 'Eagle Eagle.' You see, the foundling only knew the German word for what he was: 'Igel', which sounds exactly like 'Eagle' in English.

So Seamus, not knowing any German, set about teaching him how to be an eagle. Where they live, what they eat and how they behave. He had always been a marvellous teacher and his pupil learned quickly and well.

But the sheepdog was very old and very blind and never realised that his pupil was, in fact, a hedgehog.

In time Seamus died, leaving his eagle to carry on as best he could.

'Although,' said the Eagle, 'it's been very hard sometimes. I try to be brave but I often think I'm not a very good eagle.'

Loolagax tried to reassure him.

'You're the best eagle I've ever met.'

'Me too,' echoed Attila.

But then, neither of them had ever met an eagle before.

'I can't stand heights,' said the Eagle, trying to

smile, but it nearly turned into a sob so he snuffled about under a bush until he felt better.

'I think there's something wrong with me. I'm not right,' he said eventually.

To make him feel better, Attila quietly told him their stories and at the end, without making it sound like a Very Big Thing, suggested that he go to the Galapagos Islands with them.

'Do you think the Great Iguana could help me?'

The Eagle's little button eyes were so hopeful that they said, 'Yes, of course!'

'After all,' said Loolagax, 'none of us is quite right.'

The Eagle said, 'Oh, I'm so happy.'

Then he curled up in a ball of prickles and rolled down the hill into a puddle.

Chapter Seven

WHILE Loolagax, the Eagle and Attila passed the day, Percy D. Pond had been preparing for his journey to chase them. He changed his trousers and packed an old battered suitcase with spare braces, a Hawaiian shirt, khaki shorts and sandals. Then, going into his small kitchen, he made four tomato sandwiches, four banana sandwiches and a thermos of tea with lots of sugar. Then he baked some little cakes with sultanas in and wrapped them in greaseproof paper.

He put on his coat and bowler hat and strapped his case on to the back of his bicycle, which was green and very smart.

He mounted up ready to go.

Then he got off and went back into his cottage to make sure the gas was off, leave a note for the milkman and pick up his passport.

Then, remembering the vulture, he took his catapult out of its hiding place, for protection. He had been brilliant with it at school, the only thing he was really good at.

Then he went off to find a boat to take him to the Galapagos Islands.

It was a lovely day and Percy D. Pond cycled along whistling a little tune he had made up.

Then he saw Loolagax.

Then he fell off his bicycle.

Retrieving his bowler hat from under a sheep, he took out his catapult, loaded it with a stone and sneaking up close, took aim at Loolagax's bald head, which stood up like a periscope from behind a rock.

The stone from Pond's catapult struck the vulture on the side of his head, which made him close his eyes and lie down immediately with blood on his face.

The Eagle and Attila watched Pond approach them, up the hill, with his catapult and net at the ready. Attila didn't know what to do and stood flapping stupidly over Loolagax trying to wake him.

The Eagle was saying, over and over, 'We'll never get away. We'll never get to the Galapagos. We'll never find a home.'

Then he did something very brave. Closing his eyes and screwing up his paws he launched himself off the rocky ledge at the approaching bowler hat, making attacking eagle noises as loudly as his furry snout would allow.

He hit the back of Pond's neck at sixty-five miles an hour, knocking the man out and almost doing the same to himself.

The commotion made Loolagax wake up, and when he realised what the Eagle had done for them, even though Pond was now after him too, he flew down to see if he could help.

The Eagle was in a sorry state. Most of his prickles were bent or broken. He had one black eye and his pointed snout was wrinkled up like a concertina.

Loolagax picked him up very gently in his beak and carried him back to where the penguin waited.

They patched up their brave friend and, leaving Percy snoring in a cow pat, they started off on their journey.

They flew as before, only this time the Eagle sat on Attila's back, clinging on with all four paws and squinting against the slipstream.

Loolagax could not talk much as he was holding the key in his mouth, but he did manage to say that he was going to fly west.

This seemed a good idea. Although none of them knew where the Galapagos Islands were they were pretty sure South America was to the left of Ireland.

So on and on into the crisp dark night they flew, with the Eagle singing Irish and German songs to keep their spirits up.

Chapter Eight

BACK in the cow pat Percy D. Pond sat and cried. He was very depressed, so he ate a tomato sandwich and felt a bit better. It was now very dark and although he was supposed to be a bad person he was very frightened and he couldn't find his bicycle, which upset him because he loved it very much.

He jumped out of his skin when a voice close to him said, 'Is this what you're looking for?'

Percy struck a match to see the voice's owner by.

He burned his fingers but saw the sinister outline of Mochin Accord before he dropped the match.

He felt Accord's arm heavy on his shoulders.

'My dear Pond.'

The arm seemed heavier.

'You are undoubtedly the most stupid, fat, short-sighted idiot it has ever been my misfortune to employ. What do you think?'

Pond frowned with concentration, trying to decide what the right answer would be, but Accord saved him the trouble of replying by taking hold of the brim of Pond's bowler and pulling it down to his chin.

Accord ignored Pond's muffled cries for help and said, 'If you want a job done well, do it yourself.' With that he dumped Percy into the carrier of the bicycle, mounted it himself and pedalled off at top speed towards the Galapagos Islands.

Chapter Nine

Now, you may be wondering what happened to Sir Effluent Scrummage the Venerable Walrus and Lady Honoria Wette Bannister the Sea Cow, and what exactly an Iguana is and whether the lamp fish kept his date on the continental shelf. These are certainly the things that Attila wondered as they flew over the dark Atlantic by the light of the northern stars.

They flew on and on, the Eagle now on the

vulture's back, and Attila telling stories to keep Loolagax awake until Loolagax said in a very tired voice, 'I'm asleep.'

And he was.

The Eagle poked him with about fifty prickles and the vulture jerked awake, almost pulling the tips of the braces off Attila's flippers.

Attila thought if they didn't stop soon his flippers would fall off, they ached so much.

They decided to rest until dawn and, while there was no land in sight, there were plenty of odds and ends lying about on the sea that they could all curl up on.

'Look there!' peeped the Eagle. 'An island!'

In the starlight Loolagax peered down and spotted the long dark shape that the Eagle was pointing to. Assuming it to be a sandbank they prepared to land.

But it wasn't.

It wasn't an island at all.

It was oil.

Thick, black, poisonous, deadly oil.

They hit it right in the middle and in five

minutes they couldn't swim, they couldn't fly and the Eagle was starting to sink. Just his little snout stuck up above the evil black slime. Breathing in the choking fumes he whispered, 'I'm sorry, I really thought it was an island.'

Then the Eagle disappeared beneath the sludge. Loolagax tried to reach him but all his feathers were coated in oil. He too was beginning to lose the battle to stay afloat. Feebly he tried to keep his head up.

Attila stretched out to them both, overbalanced and choked as he swallowed a great lungful of oil and water.

The Eagle's paws appeared for a moment and then for the last time, slowly, slowly he sank below the rippleless surface.

At that moment there was a cry of 'Allez Ooop!' and the Eagle shot ten feet into the air followed closely by a bottle-nosed dolphin of immense charm who caught the slippery creature while skittering backwards on the tip of her tail.

Then with another cry of 'Allez Ooop!' the now tightly-rolled ball of spines was caught expertly by another grinning dolphin. All together there were thirty-two of them and in the next seven minutes they pulled, bounced, threw and jumped the Eagle, the vulture and the penguin free of oil.

When they'd rubbed and drubbed as much of the oil off themselves and their three prizes as they could, they linked up, all standing on their tails, giggling with joy.

The biggest bluest dolphin bounded over the bedraggled three, now being floated by some older, more sedate dolphins.

'Allez Ooop!' she shouted, landing out of a triple back flip in front of them. 'Presenting . . . The Flying Anaglyptas!'

As if joined by invisible strings all the dolphins did a back flip, reappearing a moment later clapping their flippers and scudding backwards on their tails. The chief dolphin, know as Aly, lay on her side smiling at the oily creatures.

'You see,' she said, 'Man is a bit of a worry.'

'Bit of a worry! Bit of a worry!' the other dolphins repeated.

'They're mucky and can't be trusted.'

'If you put a man's brains in a squid, it'd swim backwards,' interrupted a small dolphin while balancing on its nose.

'Squids do swim backwards you daft pudding,' sighed the chief Anaglypta.

She grinned again.

'Here, how'd you three like to be in our circus? You could be our speciality act.'

The dolphins laughed so much at this that they had to have a lie down, which they all did, rolling with the swell of the sea.

'Well,' said Attila, 'that's very nice of you, but we're on a mission really.'

And he explained.

Chapter Ten

WHILE the three new members of the Sea Circus got to know their saviours, Mochin Accord, Percy D. Pond and the green bicycle, Beryl, were loaded aboard a whaling ship bound for the Azores – islands where whales come together to talk and sing and meet their friends.

Mochin Accord was very pleased to be on board, because he knew that the sailors on board enjoyed killing whales and wouldn't be silly and sentimental about him catching and caging a penguin and a vulture. He didn't know about the Eagle yet. The terrible name of the terrible ship was the *Bloody Mary*.

Mochin smiled his wicked smile while the vessel got closer and closer to the dolphins' destination. They too were bound for the Azores and a party with their cousins, the whales.

Percy wasn't sure he liked the idea of killing whales with exploding harpoons, but he was confused because, working for Mochin Accord, he was supposed to be a baddy. So he had another sandwich, which had got a bit squashy by now. Then he practised looking bad by screwing his eyes up and frowning. That gave him a headache, so he fingered his catapult meaningfully and wondered about the terrible monster which had knocked him out.

Chapter Eleven

O N the other side of the Azores, two dignified humps were floating slowly toward the islands. From one came the sound of a tiny soprano voice, from the other, an occasional 'Harrumph' and the slow splosh of a barnacled flipper.

Sir Effluent and Lady Honoria had been thrown far away in the opposite direction when the storm came and had been poddling around the ocean searching for Attila ever since. As the Azores were known to be the sea world's news centre, they decided to go there.

Lady Honoria was trying to hurry the walrus along because she was worried about Attila and also that she might miss her date with Fumidor the lamp fish, but Sir Effluent was not be hurried.

'Penguins,' he rumbled, 'are small creatures.' He paused for a mile or two. 'Easily overlooked.'

Lady Honoria agreed but insisted that even a penguin would be unlikely to be found under a tasty kelp bed four fathoms down.

Chapter Twelve

ATTILA, Loolagax and the Eagle, after a short discussion, decided to join the Flying Anaglyptas for protection and guidance. They called themselves the Three Superglyptas and became a star attraction of the Sea Circus.

They practised their act, a show-off version of the Penguin Glider, with the Eagle doing some very slow and careful forward rolls on Attila's back while Loolagax flew very, very carefully. They made firm friends with the dolphin troupe who were mostly Italian, with a few Greeks who had got tired of playing with the tourists holidaying in the Aegean. Also, as both Greeks and Italians agreed:

'It's get flippin' mucky round them wetters now, in it?'

Remembering their recent experience with the oil the three friends nodded wisely on all questions of pollution.

Attila asked if the Flying Anaglyptas were going to the Azores as much to escape the 'Oppluzione' as anything else. But they just laughed and some of the younger ones shouted: 'Oppluzione! Ascolta Gianni! Oppluzione!'

Aly ignored them and explained, 'No no, not at all. You see, every year, the Flyin' Anaglyptas make the journey for to visit wi' de cousins. An this year is especil. You know for why? I tell you. It's for because every ten year iss the Three Choir Festival. And this . . .' she did a magnificent back flip '. . . iss de year.'

'You sing as well?' asked Loolagax.

'No, no, no, not to sing dolphins, not for serious.

No, the Whale Voice Choir! The best three in de Worl' esingin' now. And great soloists: Boris from Russia, Dai the Whale from Wales, and the greatest of all, Big Lucy from Palermo!' All the Italians cheered. 'Fantastic, I tell you!'

Aly was so excited at the prospect of hearing her giant cousins sing that she shot off backwards and knocked over a group practising a tricky pyramid.

The three travellers took the opportunity of a moment's peace to discuss their plan.

'We haven't got a plan,' squeaked the Eagle. 'We're just whiffling about at the mercy of the wind and sea.'

Attila and Loolagax realised it was very difficult for the little creature and politely ignored his rather petulant tone.

'I think,' said Loolagax slowly, 'that when we get to these Azores we must ask the whales how to get to the Galapagos.' Here he paused, remembering how very big even the smallest whale can be. 'I think they know how best to get to where we're going and which way we must go and . . . everything,' he finished rather lamely.

'Right,' said Attila, seeing that Loolagax was losing confidence and that the Eagle was still very unhappy. 'We'll practise our act, so as not to let the dolphins down, and when we get to the Azores something . . .' he paused to draw himself up and fill himself with confidence he wasn't sure he felt '. . . will come up!'

Chapter Thirteen

THE filthy, rusting whaling ship chugged on. Blood still caked its decks from the last murderous voyage it had made. The men in charge of the harpoon gun lovingly oiled it and tested its mechanism over and over again. Each exploding harpoon cost a lot of money and the captain employed them because they always hit the whale first shot. Never missed.

Percy hoped they might miss this time. As they

neared their destination, the weather had become very hot and clammy. Percy had rinsed his flask out and filled it with water but it was tepid when it went in and tasted very nasty.

The more uncomfortable and unhappy Pond became the more Accord enjoyed himself. He took to sitting with the captain at night, drinking and telling stories of killing and capturing things. During the day he stood at the very front of the ship, the part sailors call the prow. Percy asked Mochin Accord why he sat there. After all, it was very uncomfortable and he got wet every time the ship went through a wave.

Accord smiled his nasty smile at Percy's stupidity and said:

'I sit here because I have the sharpest eyesight on board. I'll see the animal before anyone. You know, I've never seen anything so big die before.'

The sailors weren't quite sure they liked this attitude because, although they liked working at sea, it was only a job and none of them enjoyed the killing bit.

After ten days, Mochin Accord turned from his

lookout post and, with a strange gleam in his eye, walked up to the captain.

'Excuse me,' he said, 'there is a large whale off to starboard.'

And sure enough, a couple of miles away to the right of the ship was a huge tail fluke lazily waving about above the water. The ship was immediately alive with shouts and men running. Everyone was excited, but to Percy D. Pond's horror Mochin Accord was the most excited. He was almost drooling at the thought of killing something so enormous.

Percy just wanted to hide but Accord insisted he come and stand close by the harpoon gun so he could watch the men fire it. Pond did as he always did and obeyed.

The whale in question was totally unaware of what was going on so close behind and it continued to do what it had been doing for the last hundred miles: singing scales. This whale, spotted so accurately by Mochin Accord, was probably the most famous whale in the world. He was the great Boris. The finest Russian soloist that ever sang. His voice was deeper than any before him and the tone of it smoother than a halibut's tummy. Many sea creatures favoured Big Lucy's soaring tenor voice or Dai the Whale's superb baritone, but serious students of the voice knew Boris's bass was without equal.

He had grown to an enormous size, saying with each gigantic mouthful of food, 'For the voice. Without food the voice does not answer. You understand?'

Boris was also the sweetest natured of cetaceans. Some, including his uncle Vladislav, thought him a trifle slow or 'a couple of fish short of a shoal' as he put it. But Vladislav was a killer whale and they are notoriously picky.

At the moment the harpoon was being loaded and everyone on the ship was screaming at everyone else Boris was just starting the aria that he was going to sing at the Three Choir Festival.

To get a good deep breath he rose majestically to the surface. At that moment the lookout called,

'Land ho, Azores, dead ahead!'

And a second later Mochin Accord shouted:

'There he blows! Dead ahead!'

Immediately the order was given to fire the harpoon at Boris.

In the split second it took for the sailor to pull the massive trigger Percy D. Pond, with a strange strangled cry, knocked the man's arm. The man's arm was thick and much stronger than Percy's so it only moved a tiny way, but that small movement was enough to make the harpoon go off target just enough, no more, only just enough to stop it killing Boris.

But it didn't miss him.

The harpoon scraped along Boris's back, causing him to dive because of the shock and pain, but the dive meant his huge tail fluke was right in the way of the harpoon. It hit the great waving fin and, without exploding, went straight through, leaving a huge ragged hole in Boris's beautiful tail.

On board the ship all hell was let loose. The captain was so angry he started to strangle Percy who went red, then blue, then very limp, at which point the captain dropped him on the deck with a lot of very nasty words.

Mochin Accord too was very angry with him and kicked him in an unnecessarily vicious manner, then stepped over him to speak to the captain.

'Perhaps it's not so bad,' he said reasonably, with his most charming smile. 'The whale must be injured. All we have to do is wait until it comes to the surface to breathe.' He paused. 'Or die,' he added quietly and with relish.

Percy D. Pond lay on the floor of that stinking boat and thought that he was more lonely and unhappy than ever he had been in the whole of his lonely and unhappy life. Nobody had ever told him that doing a good thing, when everyone round you is doing bad things, can make you feel like that.

Under the sea, in the deep blackness of the deep black water, Boris summoned all his strength and began to sing.

He sang as never before. The voice was dark and rich but melancholy and yearning as singing can only be when the singer knows what it is to suffer not just for one lifetime but for many generations.

Almost a hundred miles in each direction the

heart-rending notes echoed through the sea, into caves, under rocks and into the shells of creatures who cried at the desolate sound.

The Flying Anaglyptas heard it and silence fell on them like a stone.

Attila, Loolagax and Eagle didn't know what the sound was. Aly, listening intently, said slowly, as if translating, 'Is distress song. A cousin – Great Whale – is dying . . . Maybe no, no is not possible! Is Boris!'

'Oh, no, not Boris! Not Cousin Boris!'

It began quietly but all at once the dolphins were screaming with anger and concern. Within a moment they had formed themselves into a group ready to set off to rescue and avenge.

'Just a minute,' shouted Loolagax over the hubbub, 'you could do with some air power, reconnaissance and all that. We'll come with you.'

'It's not your fight, bird, not your friend,' said one of the old dolphins. 'Our family has been persecuted for centuries by men with harpoons. It's our fight.'

Attila interrupted.

'None of us is safe. If it isn't harpoons it's oil, or nets, or that they think there are too many of us. There's no creature that can say it's my fight or it's not my fight any more!'

The little penguin suddenly looked very dignified and not at all comical. Nobody laughed or said he didn't know what he was talking about. The dolphins just nodded and opened their ranks for the friends to join them as they swam faster than they had ever swum towards the melancholy singing.

Loolagax flew above like a fighter going to war.

Chapter Fourteen

SOME miles in the opposite direction a great tusked head broke the surface with a cry.

'Barnacled Bottoms, it's Boris's song! What have those boatsmen done to him?'

Lady Honoria surfaced a little way from Sir Effluent.

'Boris? Not the Great Boris,' she cried. 'Well don't just float there, we must help him.' Sir Effluent opened his mouth to speak but Lady Honoria went on.

'Remember when my sister got caught in those drift nets? Boris swam right into them, tore them up so she could go free. He still has the scars where those horrible nets wrapped around him and cut into him for weeks until a swordfish did the decent thing.'

She paused. The walrus was amazed. He had never seen her so stirred up.

'We must DO SOMETHING!!!!' she bellowed.

'Right ho!' said Sir Effluent.

He drew himself up, puffed out his enormous chest and with a great disturbance of the inky water, plunged off, followed by Lady Honoria, to save Boris.

Chapter Fifteen

ABOUT an hour later the harpoon gun was reloaded and all was quiet on the whaler.

Percy had crawled into a corner and was praying no one would remember he was there.

Mochin Accord and the sailors watched the still sea for a sign of Boris surfacing.

All was quiet. Ominously quiet.

On the ocean bottom Boris knew he could hold out no longer, he would have to surface for breath, his voice was weakening at last and he was feeling very faint through loss of blood.

Worst of all, through the gloom he could see the sharks beginning to gather.

Slowly, slowly he began drifting to the surface.

Like nightmare shadows the sharks drifted with him, silently waiting until they knew he could not fight back.

Then suddenly, out of the still silence, everything happened at once. The sharks moved in like lightning as the sun broke through the surface of the water. With teeth bared for ripping and shredding flesh, they closed in a circle around Boris.

At the same moment, like the breaking of a thousand glasses, the dolphins dropped out of the sky. One phenomenal leap out from the shadow of the ship and they had taken the sharks completely by surprise. The dolphins, bigger and cleverer, poked and punched the sharks. The sharks fought back with superior speed and their terrible teeth.

On the surface, Loolagax flew in low and fast, launching the Eagle, now a ball of lethal spines, into the face of the captain.

Attila hit the harpoon man like a javelin in the back of the neck and Loolagax, remembering everything his father had taught him, went like a thing demented for the eyes of Mochin Accord.

The sailors ran about in confusion. Several of them thought the devil had come on board and others thought Loolagax was an albatross and so refused to shoot him as it is very, very unlucky to harm an albatross.

Percy D. Pond could not believe his eyes. He began to stagger towards the centre of the chaos, to save Mochin Accord from Loolagax, but something was holding him back.

Little teeth were embedded in the bottom of Percy's trousers. Paws were slipping on the wet deck. Something that looked uncommonly like a hedgehog was trying to stop him! At the same time a small penguin was pecking the shin bone of his other leg. Pond stopped.

He looked down and thought for a moment that these two and the mad vulture might be trying to – no, it was too ridiculous.

Percy kicked the penguin off. Attila shot across the slippery floor like a deck quoit and only stopped when he hit a huge coil of rope. Percy then bent down to try to get rid of the Eagle but soon stopped when he felt how sharp his spines were. Looking at the chaos in front of him, Percy thought it might not be a bad idea to let himself be pulled away.

Mochin Accord suddenly screamed out in a terrible voice, 'The whale! The whale! It's surfacing! Harpoon it! Kill it! Kill it now!'

Loolagax, who'd been doing quite well up till then, was grabbed by his long neck by one of the sailors and pulled off Accord.

'Don't wring its neck yet – I want to do it myself. Then I'll have it stuffed and we'll eat it for dinner,' said Accord quickly before he turned back to watch Boris.

The harpoon was ready and Boris's huge back was now clearly visible in the bright sunlight.

He blew all the old air and water out of his lungs through his blow hole and it looked like a rainbow fountain.

'Fire! Fire dammit! What's stopping you, you idiots?'

The captain signalled to the harpoonist, who pulled the trigger.

Nothing happened.

He pulled it again.

Nothing.

Mochin Accord, hysterical now in case they lost the kill, pushed the sailor out of the way and pulled the trigger himself.

Each time the trigger was pulled, it released a bolt that was supposed to hit another bolt and set off the gunpowder which would fire the harpoon.

But a small penguin had climbed up and put his flipper between the bolts so it wouldn't fire and, even though it was agony every time the bolt struck, like having a door shut on your finger, Attila didn't move.

No one on board had spotted what he'd done when suddenly, as if from under the ship, a gigantic blue whale rose up, then another appeared on the left of the ship, then another on the right, then one behind. They closed in on the hull until the ship couldn't move forward backwards or sideways. Then more and more whales appeared, all different, minke and killer, sperm and humpback, until it seemed the sea had become hilly land.

Then all the hills began to sing, in harmonies so deep that the very iron of the ship's hull began to vibrate. The whole ship shook with the sound of the singing of the North Atlantic Whale Voice Choir.

Beneath the water the sharks found themselves batted casually about like toy balls. They were tossed back and forth from barnacled flipper to barnacled flipper by whales unseen on the surface. Those sharks that could swam for their lives. The rest waited until the whales had finished with them, then, nursing their wounds, slunk away.

After a little while the vibrations of the choir's singing began to loosen the rivets and bolts holding the ship together.

The frightened people on board watched as the ship started to disintegrate. As the hand rails broke up so men fell screaming into the water.

The whales did not harm them. Neither did they help them. Now the vessel collapsed completely with a scream of steam and men. Only the wooden deck floated, with Mochin Accord and Percy clinging to it. With a flick of his tail, Fluke, the lead tenor, broke it into matchsticks.

Luckily, the three friends, who were bobbing about in the water, were spotted by Aly, who, despite terrible wounds from the battle with the sharks, managed to alert the whales to the danger that Loolagax, Attila and the Eagle were in.

At that, the blue whale who'd first stopped the ship, whose eye was bigger than all three of them and who was so big they never managed to see all of him at once, sank beneath them and then rose with them on his back.

They stood on their own vast island surrounded by happy triumphant whales who started a new song. And the back on which they stood hummed too with happiness and triumph.

Chapter Sixteen

HELICOPTERS and boats had been sent out from
the Azores to rescue the whale boat's crew.
Mochin Accord, pulling Percy by the scruff of the
neck, forced his way on board the first rescue
helicopter.

Because he was very rich he soon found someone
on dry land with a plane. Mochin Accord gave
the man a lot of money, and the man, whose name

was Matteo, said he could take him and Percy to follow the whales.

And so they continued to chase the vulture, the penguin and the Eagle across the world, but now Mochin Accord just wanted to kill them and as many whales as he could.

Leaving the Three Choir Festival reluctantly, the younger whales and the least wounded dolphins set out to get the three friends to the east coast of South America, where Loolagax was sure that he had relations who might help them.

The Whale Voice Choir sang as they left, a song of thanks and farewell, the voices of Big Lucy, Dai and of course the Great Boris ringing through all others in wonderful harmonies. Finally Big Lucy sang a solo, almost bursting a blood vessel he was so proud, grateful and happy.

Attila was thrilled but puzzled.

'Why is he called Lucy? He's a he isn't he?' he whispered to Aly.

The dolphin smothered her giggles. 'Of course he is. 'is name is Luciano but everyone call 'im Big Lucy.'

Attila tried to look as if he wasn't surprised.

Eventually the singing stopped. The three friends were sad to go as it was the biggest and most wonderful party and a lot of it was in honour of Loolagax, Attila and the Eagle, but they had tides to catch and hurricanes to miss.

Sir Effluent and Lady Honoria, who'd arrived just in time to see the sharks defeated, listened to Attila tell them the whole story and told him there was no time to swim around the bottom of Argentina and up to the Galapagos as Mochin Accord was bound to follow, and anyway the storms were raging around Tierra de Fuego like the pictures on treasure maps.

So, having advised the dolphins to drop the three friends somewhere south of Venezuela, the walrus and the sea cow said they'd meet them later at the Galapagos as they could not travel overland but would try to get through the Panama canal after Lady Honoria had kept her date with Fumidor.

Chapter Seventeen

THE dolphins and whales swam fast and straight, always staying on the surface in order to keep their precious passengers as dry as possible. Which is to say completely soaked through, but dry by sea-life standards.

As the group approached the shallows off Venezuela, thousands of birds flocked to greet them. Most of them were just looking for fish scattered by the approaching whales and were quite rude, diving in and out of the water without so much as a 'good morning', but they were mostly cormorants who are known to have bad manners. A lot of the gulls were friendly though and gave them a screaming escort towards the shore.

The sea was rough and the three friends saw there was no way to get safely to the beach.

Loolagax could have flown alone but he could not take his companions as they had no way of setting up the glider and no runway to take off from.

After swimming hundreds of miles the whales and dolphins were tired and bitterly disappointed. All they wanted was to go home and rest, but none of them would abandon Loolagax, Attila and the Eagle.

Attila shouted over the wind that he'd try to swim, and Loolagax was about to say he'd carry the Eagle in his beak, when the wet ball of prickles said, as loud as he could, 'I'm an eagle. I'll fly. I'll be all right.'

For a moment there was astonished silence, then the whales started to laugh, deep rolling laughter.

Then the dolphins joined in. Great joyous whoops.

'Why are they laughing? What did I say? Are they laughing at me?'

Attila patted him and said, 'No, no, not at you, Eagle. They're not laughing at you.'

Two more mature dolphins, shushing the others, swam close to the whale on which the three were riding.

'Don't take any notice of my friends. They are just over tired,' said the larger dolphin, grinning his kind, dolphin smile.

'Come on,' said the other, 'we'll give you a lift to the shore.'

'But it's too shallow,' Attila blurted out.

'We'll be all right. After all we're the Flying Anaglyptas!' they shouted in unison, standing on their tails.

Transferring the three friends on to the dolphins' backs from the huge heights of the whales was difficult, and finally they decided that sliding off into the sea and then the dolphins coming up under them would be the easiest way. Easy enough for the penguin, he happily jumped into the waves, swam around for a while like a dart, then reappeared leaning against the dorsal fin of Finn, the handsome dolphin who'd stopped the others laughing at the Eagle, who was to go next.

The Eagle trusted the whales and the dolphins and was no more than a bit scared when he rolled off into the sea. Once he felt the dolphin's back under him he unrolled so as not to hurt her with his spines.

Everybody knew it would be worst for Loolagax. Once his feathers were waterlogged he was so heavy he couldn't keep his head out of the water.

He was very, very frightened and thought perhaps he could fly across to the dolphin, but as he spread his wings he realised they felt as heavy as lead. He jumped to try to give himself lift but immediately fell into the water which seemed to force itself into his mouth and down his throat, making him cough and choke.

Just as he thought he was finished, the third dolphin lifted him up and held him steady, gently blowing air over his sodden feathers.

The dolphins, chattering and whistling to each

other, not for fun but to tell each other where the dangerous rocks were and if there were any jelly fish about, swam through the huge waves towards the silvery shore.

A couple of times they thought they heard the noise of a plane's propellor, but the wind was blowing and the sea was shouting so they couldn't be sure, and the sky stayed clear blue with no black shadows.

They were now close enough to the beach to make a run at dropping off the friends. This was the hardest part, for the dolphins had to get close enough to throw their passengers clear on to the sand, but not so close that they might get stranded themselves.

First was Loolagax. He was thrown quite a long way up the beach and his dolphin, Blow, turned for safety with a triumphant flick of his tail.

Next, Finn flipped Attila into the shallows from where he made his own way up the shingle to join Loolagax. Finn swam off with a dolphin laugh.

Nobody really saw what happened next, but the Eagle found himself safe and dry on the beach.

Bruised and dazed, Loolagax stood up and ruffled his broken feathers. All three of the friends were safe, though shaken. But at the water's edge a dolphin lay still. Out of the water her blue-grey skin was drying in the fierce sun. Her dolphin grin looked out of place next to the pain in her eyes. In trying to make sure the Eagle was safe, she'd swum too close to the shore.

The friends rushed to her.

'We must get her back into the water. She's beached. She can't get back on her own, she's too heavy out of the water,' the Eagle shouted. He had seen many dolphins stranded and dying on the beach near his home. He knew that without the sea their friend would die. Frantically he pushed the huge body. In the sea the other dolphins called and whistled but could come no closer.

'Move, please move!' the Eagle squeaked. 'Help her, Loolagax. Attila, help!' They all pushed, but it was no good. The tide was going out and the sea moved further away from the still dolphin.

'Stop now,' she whispered. 'It's no good. But thank you, my friends. Good luck on your journey.'

Her eyes closed. The Eagle pricked her hard to wake her up. Slowly, her eyes opened again and a tear rolled down her long snout.

'Eagle, Eagle. You're braver and better than any eagle.' The little spiny creature strained to hear her. 'But you're not an eagle. You're a hedgehog. A dear kind hedgehog, the noblest of animals.'

And, in spite of the pulling and prodding of Loolagax, Attila and the Eagle she closed her eyes and died.

Chapter Eighteen

THE scream of an aeroplane's engines shattered the silence and Mochin Accord was spraying the beach with bullets. Percy D. Pond could not get close enough to jog his arm this time.

The friends thought they would be killed for sure but, frightened by the noise of the plane, thousands of sea birds flew up from the sea and rocks, right into its path.

The pilot panicked, because if one of the birds was sucked into the engines, the plane would stall and crash into the cliffs. He pulled it up and away from the wheeling flocks of birds.

Mochin Accord was thrown backwards, and down the beach the three friends ran for their lives. They ran to the rocks and into a crack in the cliff face. Exhausted, they collapsed in a heap of feathers and spines.

The plane's engines screamed and faded. Soon all they could hear was the distant whoosh of the surf.

Attila tried a little laugh which didn't work.

'Well, what are we going to do now?'

The Eagle wasn't listening.

'Poor dolphin. She was so kind. But . . . but . . . is it true? Am I a – what was it?'

'Hedgehog,' said Attila softly. 'Yes, it's true. The bit about being noble was true too. Like a lion.'

'What's a lion?' asked the Eagle.

'Look, a cousin!' Loolagax shattered the quiet and flew three feet into the air, coming down in a shower of sand and feathers. The vulture was staring up into the shadows, making excited squawks. As their eyes got used to the dark they saw a figure looming above them.

It was like Loolagax in shape but bigger, much, much bigger. Its beak was curved and crooked, as if it had been carved out of iron. Glimmering black eyes stared down at them unblinking.

'Si! Primo. Soy tu primo! Cousin! I am your cousin, vulture.'

The bird spread his black wings. None of them had ever seen wings so big. Attila gasped and looked at his flippers.

The big bird made a rasping noise with his vicious beak. After a moment they realised he was giggling and showing off his wing feathers.

'They are a bit good, aren't they? Biggest in our family.'

He hopped down level with them and leaned towards them conspiratorially.

'You see . . . they're for flying.'

It occurred to all three friends that, actually, although the big bird was impressive and obviously strong, he was a bit, just a little bit, simple.

'And look,' he went on, 'when I flap them they make all the dust jump about.'

He swept his huge wings a couple of times and made a small sandstorm.

'Good, isn't it?'

The sand was almost covering the Eagle, so Loolagax took charge.

'You're a condor, aren't you? The Bird of the High Andes. You fly over mountain ranges and people write songs about you because you're the Magical Bird of South America.'

The condor paused in his flapping.

'Yeh, that's me. Cotomotitipaxi. But my friends call me Max. I tell you what, though.'

The razor beak leant dangerously close to the Eagle's button nose.

'A lot of creatures are frightened of me. Don't know why. So I don't have that many friends. Shame really, 'cos I like a laugh. Here, have you heard the one about the llama and the parrot?'

The condor then told them a long joke that they didn't understand. They laughed politely though, and he was delighted.

'You liked that one, did you? Right then, here's a good one – what do you call a llama with his head in a bucket?' He paused a second. 'Anything you like. He can't hear you!'

The condor laughed until he cried. Under the noise Attila whispered to the Eagle:

'What's a llama?'

The Eagle shrugged. 'A humpless camel that looks like a tall goat, I think.' The penguin looked doubtful.

'So,' Max was suddenly serious. 'What's the problem? Qué pasa hombres? What are you three hiding from? Dígame! Tell Maxie.'

The three friends couldn't be sure that the condor understood the whole story, but at the end of it he wrapped his vast wings around them and shouted:

'Don't worry, Maxie's here. Tell you what I'll do. I'll take you over the other side. I'll take you to the coast of Ecuador, although,' here he shuddered and lowered his voice, 'I'm not going over the wet bit. If I fell in I'd never get out.' Suddenly Max bounced up in the air, full of enthusiasm. 'Ay, caramba! I've got an idea. My friend Franklin. Franklin will take you to the Galapagos Islands. He can visit his Auntie. I think his Auntie has no seen him for half a century at least. Yes. Franklin will take you!'

Chapter Nineteen

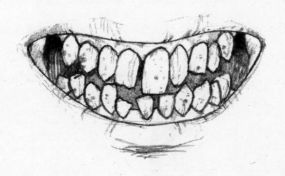

As the condor rose into the sky with Attila and the Eagle on his back and Loolagax flying behind, Mochin Accord watched them through binoculars.

In a moment he was back in the plane. The pilot made a steep take off and Percy was sick into a paper bag.

'Follow that condor,' said Mochin Accord to the pilot. 'This time I'll get them.'

He smiled and showed his horrible teeth.

Chapter Twenty

THE condor flew on and on, his massive wings beating time to a song he sang for hours on end. After the sun had gone down and come up again over a range of snowy mountains, Loolagax admitted defeat and gave up flying. Now he sat on Maxie's back with the others. The great bird never seemed to tire.

They flew over lakes and impossibly high

waterfalls, over deep valleys and vast forests. They flew through heat and cold, and tasted salt and snow in the air.

The bitter wind made talking impossible, so each of the three friends was alone with his thoughts and the beauty of the purple sky.

After another day they saw the sea on the other side of South America. The mountains of the Andes got smaller and the ocean got bigger, until all they could see was the rocky shore and the endless blue water.

Chapter Twenty-One

FAR above them in the cockpit of the plane, Mochin Accord watched the distant dot flying towards the coast, without blinking.

'Galapagos! Nearly there. Then I've got you trapped,' he muttered.

Pond opened his eyes.

'What did you say, sir?'

'Land over there,' Mochin said to the pilot, 'and you, Pond, when we're down get me a fast boat and a large strong net. I've got the gun.'

He patted it lovingly. Pond blinked. How was he going to ask for a boat and a net when he didn't speak Spanish? Life was even more difficult than he had feared.

Chapter Twenty-Two

MAX thumped down on to the boulders of the shore.

'Sorry, my legs have gone to sleep. Hop off.'

The three friends tumbled, cramped, off the condor's back. They thanked him in every way they could and Max was very happy, especially when Loolagax said, 'You may be my cousin, but we are your friends. If there's ever anything we can do . . .'

The condor butted in embarrassed, 'Yes, yes, never mind about all that. Be nice if you came over for a visit now and then though. Now where's Franklin?'

He looked about a bit then shouted, 'Franklin! Franklin! Dónde estás? Franklin!'

He paused, then said, 'Ah . . . here he is. Franklin, hombre, how you doing?'

The three friends couldn't see who the condor was talking to, in fact they looked at each other and were all wondering if Maxie had had too much sun.

Then they saw Franklin. On the far side of the cove in which they stood, a boulder was moving, dragging itself slowly, oh so slowly, towards them.

As it got closer they saw it had a shovel-like foot at each corner, covered in scales and tipped with long, curved nails. Its long wrinkled neck didn't seem to have a head on the end of it, just a face of ancient green leather with bright, mischievous eyes and a wide smile. He didn't have ears or eyebrows, just two little holes for a nose. Every now and then he opened his mouth wide, showing a stumpy pink tongue, and tore off a juicy bit of greenery from the scrubby bushes.

When Franklin got close to them, Attila realised he wasn't a boulder but the biggest sea turtle he'd ever seen, not that he'd seen many. Loolagax and the Eagle, of course, had never seen one and were speechless.

The Eagle whispered to Loolagax, 'Do you think he's a dinosaur?'

'Probably,' said Loolagax, not taking his eyes off Franklin.

The turtle heaved himself to a halt in front of the condor and stretched his long, old neck up to see him, then spoke in a voice rich with laughter and the rum of the Caribbean.

'Good to see you, Maxie! Didn't hear you land, man. I bin sleeping since November so it's nice to be wakin' up to you. Who's this you brought to see me Maxie?'

Maxie immediately did the introductions, although he couldn't remember Attila's name and thought the Eagle was a young porcupine, but apart from that he did very well.

'So what's the story?' asked Franklin, settling down to chew some seaweed.

Attila, after glancing at the others, told their story, although he was frequently interrupted by Franklin saying things like: 'Never trust a shark. Even if it is small it will always be spiteful,' and 'I remember Boris when he was a boy soprano'. Eventually Attila got to the end, saying:

' . . . So all we have to do now is get to the Galapagos Islands and not get caught by Mochin Accord.'

'And that's where I come in, eh?' Franklin chortled. 'Don't you worry, Maxie knows I won't be letting you down. See, I'm a hundred and three years old now, but when I was just a soft shell thing I was playing in the water near Barbados – you know Barbados? Lovely island, where I was born – and I was taken up and shipped off with about a dozen of me best friends. We was put in a tank, all one on top of the other and the ones at the bottom couldn't breathe; I don't want to say what happen to them. After days in the dark with no food and all cramped up, I was put in a bucket and taken to a restaurant where they said they were going to make soup out of me. Soup! They were going to boil me up and use me beautiful shell as a soap dish! What you think of that?

'Anyway, in the night time I climb out of the bucket and walk down to the sea. But it's not the Caribbean, the lovely warm sea I know, it's this sea, big and rough and I don't know it. Nobody wanted to know me here because I was different. It was a bad time for me. So I'll help you, 'cos I know how it feels not to be wanted, I'll get you to the Galapagos Islands.' He laughed suddenly, slapping his shell with his paddle foot. 'I got an Auntie there, she's maybe two hundred years old but she don't live in the sea – she live on the land! Strange place, the Islands. Strange place!'

Franklin then took them up the beach, out of the wind, where they had something to eat and rested before they set off.

There was plenty of room for all three of them on Franklin's shell but, as it was domed and very smooth it was a bit difficult to stay on. At last the ancient turtle suggested they put some sap from a local cactus on their bottoms.

'Don't worry! It's sticky and it'll stick you to me shell. Then you won't slide off! Mind you, you might get ants in your pants 'cos they love the stuff! Hah!'

He thought this was hilarious and disappeared inside his shell laughing.

Maxie watched the three friends making a real mess of getting the sap. Attila was stabbed by the cactus spines so the Eagle attacked the cactus with his prickles. Then his prickles got stuck in the plant and he had to be pulled off by Loolagax.

Eventually the three friends had the sticky sap all over their bottoms. They climbed on board Franklin, where they stuck fast.

'I suppose we worry about how to get off when we get there,' whispered the Eagle to Loolagax, who nodded but still looked a bit worried.

It took Franklin quite a long time to drag himself down to the water, but once he was in it, his great weight disappeared and his shovel feet became superb swimming flippers. They were off.

Almost too late they realised they hadn't said goodbye to Maxie, so they shouted their love and thanks to him as he rose majestically into the air.

'Have a good trip, amigos. Hasta la proxima vez. Until the next time! Until the next time!'

The wind carried his voice away, but they waved and shouted until he disappeared into the mountains on his way back home.

Chapter Twenty-Three

MOCHIN Accord and Percy D. Pond had found a boat. A bright yellow speedboat that cut through the sea like a knife.

Accord sat down with the man who owned it and they drank a lot of stuff that tasted like drain cleaner to Percy while they haggled about the cost of hiring it.

Percy dug out his last sandwich and sultana cake, sat down in the shade and ate them sadly. His thermos was empty and he was thirsty, but he thought he'd rather wait for a cup of tea than drink the stuff Accord was drinking.

Chapter Twenty-Four

FRANKLIN swam fast and straight towards the Galapagos Islands which they soon saw surrounded by a slight mist.

'Is that them?' squeaked the Eagle.

Attila didn't say anything, but he hoped so, he was really tired and just wanted their travels to stop for a while.

The Islands seemed to grow bigger as they got

closer, and soon they could see the rocks on the shore. But what astonished them was the amount of creatures there were everywhere. In the sea shoals of flying fish jumped out of the water to have a look at them. Seals floated by as if sunbathing. Birds dived in and out of the sea and roosted in their thousands on the cliffs above. Everywhere there was movement, and everyone said hallo and welcome to them. At first they thought it was because they knew Franklin but they soon realised it was to welcome them. There seemed to be no more space for any more creatures but the Galapagans just moved up to make room for them.

'Halloo! Welcome! Look! Look! Newcomers! Welcome!' screamed the gulls.

Slowly the three friends realised that all the animals they saw were very slightly different from any they'd seen before. Everybody on the Galapagos was, indeed, different.

Franklin heaved up the shingly beach and was mobbed by friends who also hugged and kissed Attila, Loolagax and the Eagle. They unstuck themselves from Franklin's shell and slid on to the rough sand.

Loolagax was offered a piece of meat by a bird that might or might not have been from his family. The vulture was covered in confusion. He felt terrible. He didn't know what to do.

Attila, seeing his friend's unhappiness, said, 'Excuse me – he's a vegetarian.'

Normally this would have been met with a stunned and horrified silence, but to the friends' astonishment the bird just turned to a vegetarian finch and said: 'The vulture – I'm sorry, I don't know your name –'

'Loolagax.'

'– Loolagax doesn't like meat. Could he have a bit of your fruit, please?'

'Of course! Of course!'

Loolagax found himself sharing a delicious pile of figs with the finch.

The Eagle looked around in wonder.

'We're normal here. Just ordinary.'

He stopped, not believing that it could be true.

'That's good isn't it?' he asked hopefully.

'Yes . . . I think so,' said Attila hesitantly. It was all too confusing for a very small penguin.

Then the seals came rolling through the waves to greet Franklin, who was a great favourite with everyone. They all greeted the friends as if they'd just been away for a while.

On the rugged land the blue-footed, red-footed and masked boobies stood together with the mother seals and their big-eyed babies. Leaf-toed geckoes skittered around the legs of magnificent frigatebirds and lava lizards chatted with hood mockingbirds. And among them like statues, dotted among the chattering, squealing mass, stood hundreds of iguanas.

They were bow-legged, with long reptile tails, and their dragon faces were not smiling. They had serious faces, a little bit frightening to the friends who had never seen anything like them before. Silently the iguanas flicked out their long red tongues. Franklin knew his passengers were nervous so he said, 'Now then. Don't mind the iguanas. They're just not as light-minded as everyone else. Right? They are the wisdom of the

117

Islands. It's their job to love all living things and make us remember the importance of the lives we've got. They get and give Respect.'

Franklin was now dragging himself up the shingly beach towards a giant tortoise who was calling to him.

'Franklin?'

'Auntie! Auntie!'

'Franklin? Is that you? Come closer, me eyes aren't what they were . . .'

For a moment the three friends stood, unsure what to do, then a beautiful voice spoke above them.

Like the parting of water all the animals on the shore moved back and there, standing quite alone, was the Great Iguana.

It was no bigger than the others but somehow didn't look like any of them. No one knew whether the Great Iguana was male or female, no one knew its age, only that it was older than five hundred years.

Its skin was deep burnished ebony black, its flicking tongue deep crimson.

Attila stumbled forward.

'Great Iguana, I have a letter from Herbert Langoustine. You see, we've been all around the world, and there was a terrible man and – '

'I know,' the beautiful voice said, 'I have followed reports of your progress. You are very brave. All of you.'

They mumbled thank you and then fell silent. Attila handed over the tattered letter of introduction from Herbert Langoustine. The Great Iguana's dragon face seemed to smile as it said, 'A penguin who feels the cold, a vulture who won't eat meat and a hedgehog who lived as a bird. There are no others exactly like you. Each one of us here has no like anywhere. At our table in the Galapagos there is room for everyone. You know the rules already. Don't laugh at or be cruel to any other creature, and remember you are free. But remember too, your freedom stops where another's begins.'

'Grab the penguin and the others!'

Mochin Accord's voice smashed through the quiet and sent panic through the creatures. He

119

fired his gun into the crowd of blue-footed boobies, making them fly up in a confused cloud. Mochin Accord screamed at Percy D. Pond again.

'Throw the net, you damned fool!'

So Percy threw the heavy net. He threw it with all his strength . . . over Mochin Accord.

'Get me out of this, you idiot!' Accord screamed.

Percy stepped forward and said quietly, 'No. No, I won't do it. I've had enough of your cruelty and wickedness. You'll have to shoot me.'

'How can I, you numb head, I can't get out of this net! Idiot! Fool! Release me.'

Percy, having been very brave, didn't know what to do next and just stood there looking at the flailing Mochin Accord.

Slowly the iguanas, the birds, the seals and all the other creatures gathered round Accord. Their cries of welcome and shouts of laughter he heard as growls and threats. The more he twisted and struggled the louder they laughed and the more angry he got.

The Great Iguana finally silenced the laughter.

'Don't frighten him any more.'

Pond was surprised to find he understood the Great Iguana's words.

'Er . . . excuse me, sir. He's not frightened, he's angry.'

The beautiful voice sounded sad.

'It is very often the same thing.'

'Ah,' said Percy, nodding as if he knew what the Great Iguana was talking about.

'Set him free,' the Great Iguana continued. 'If he wants to stay among us he will be welcome. If not – Franklin? Would you take him back to the mainland?'

'Sure, sure thing.'

Everyone watched while the iguanas tore away the net with their claws and teeth. Accord thought he was being attacked and tried to beat them off.

When he was finally free he raised the gun with a cry of, 'I'll teach you, you –'

But he didn't finish what he was going to say because a massively fat sea lion which had flumped up behind him knocked the gun out of his hand, then, as Accord overbalanced, gently sat on him to stop him causing any more trouble.

'Well done, Dumper! Well done!' everyone shouted, at which Dumper, the sea lion, giggled like a pup.

Poor Mochin Accord was convinced the animals were trying to kill him, even though Percy tried to tell him the truth. Eventually Percy shrugged and allowed his boss to be loaded on to Franklin's back, where Accord clung, petrified of falling off and drowning.

'Move up Mr Accord, I'd better come too.' Percy moved sadly towards the sea turtle when the beautiful voice stopped him.

'Percy, you don't have to go if you don't want to. Mochin Accord is beyond help; he sees evil where there's good and enemies where there are only friends. I think perhaps you'd be more at home here than with Accord and his type. You don't really belong with them, do you?'

'But . . .' Percy stopped, not sure how to say what he meant. 'But I've done some really bad things.'

'You just saved many lives. You're not like them,' said the Great Iguana gently.

'Um . . . well . . . I'd like to stay if you wouldn't mind.'

Nobody minded and everyone shouted their happiness.

But Attila, Loolagax and the Eagle said nothing. They just watched.

A moment later Franklin set off with Mochin Accord screaming threats and insults on his back.

Chapter Twenty-Five

LIFE on the beach soon returned to normal and the three friends were introduced to everyone then left to relax in the shade with some food.

A little distance away Percy D. Pond was sitting alone, holding his bowler hat and gazing sadly out to sea.

'We ought to speak to him,' said Attila at last. 'After all, it wasn't his fault really. I'm sure he's good inside like the Great Iguana said.'

'Yes,' agreed Loolagax, but it was the Eagle who actually went over to him.

'Hallo. I'm a hedgehog, but I don't know what hedgehogs do because I was brought up as an eagle.'

'That's quite hard. I used to have hedgehogs in my garden. I liked them,' said Percy, shyly.

The Eagle nodded, not knowing what to say next. Percy looked very sad.

'Maybe,' said the Eagle shyly, 'maybe you could teach me about hedgehogs? You see, I've spent my whole life thinking I'm something I'm not.' He paused, then added quietly, 'A bit like you, really.'

Percy D. Pond's chubby face went red. He couldn't believe the Eagle was being so kind to him. Percy was suddenly happier than he could remember being for a long time. He wasn't used to people being nice to him and wasn't quite sure what he should do so he just said, 'Oh . . . that's very kind. Yes. Yes please! I'd like to tell you all I know about hedgehogs.'

What was almost a soppy moment was broken by

a jet of water and a loud cry of, 'Little chap, you got here!'

Sir Effluent and Lady Honoria were rounding the bay, shouting and laughing among the leaping Flying Anaglyptas. Close behind them, singing in harmonies too many to count, came the North Atlantic Whale Voice Choir.

The sea boiled with happiness. Whales and dolphins leaped over seals and walruses. Everyone was laughing and playing in the waves.

The iguanas did stately dances on the rocks. Percy picked up the Eagle and kissed him on the end of his snout which made him curl up in a delighted ball of spines.

In the chaos, after the penguin had almost been squeezed flat with hugs from Sir Effluent and Lady Honoria, Loolagax sat down with Attila. They were so happy they couldn't speak. But they remembered all the friends who'd helped them and particularly the beautiful dolphin who'd died and her lovely smile.

After a while of thinking and remembering they were swept up into the party. Fumidor the lamp fish was tangoing with his beloved sea cow, the walrus was tapping his tusks in time to the music, and the singing, dancing, laughter and fun went on late into the night.

Above it all the Great Iguana watched, nodding and tapping his tail to the music.

THE Galapagos Islands remain protected from people like Mochin Accord, so I suppose Attila, Loolagax, the Eagle and Percy D. Pond are happily living there still, surrounded by all their many friends, and watched over by the Great Iguana.